To Luca. —M.C.

Text and illustrations copyright © 2022 by Marianna Coppo.
All rights reserved. No part of this book may be reproduced in any form
without written permission from the publisher.

Library of Congress Cataloging-in-Publication Data available.

ISBN 978-1-7972-0442-0

Manufactured in China.

Design by Lydia Ortiz.
English translation by Debbie Bibo.
Typeset in Brandon Grotesque.
The illustrations in this book were rendered in tempera and pastels.

10 9 8 7 6 5 4 3 2 1

Chronicle Books LLC
680 Second Street
San Francisco, California 94107

Chronicle Books—we see things differently.
Become part of our community at www.chroniclekids.com.

a brave cat

By Marianna Coppo

chronicle books · san francisco

This is a box.

Inside, there's Olivia.

Olivia is an adventurer.

A tireless traveler.

A fearless explorer.

And a hunter,
through and through.

More or less.

Her life is definitely demanding.

Filled with danger.

But it's worth it.

Olivia can reach the top of the world and take it all in with a glance.

(It's actually not that hard.)

What more could
anyone ask for?

Well, it isn't as if Olivia loves everything in her life.

Take this cup, for example.   And this,   and this,

and even this
right here.

Ah,
that's more like it!

A perfect world.

Small, perhaps,
but what's wrong with that?

Come out
of the box?
But, why?

Olivia has everything she needs right here.

And they need her.

Without Olivia, their days wouldn't even begin.

Besides, from what she's seen,
the world outside isn't all
that it's cracked up to be.

The world outside is for cats
without any imagination.

And to think that there are people who still say
that cats always land on their feet!

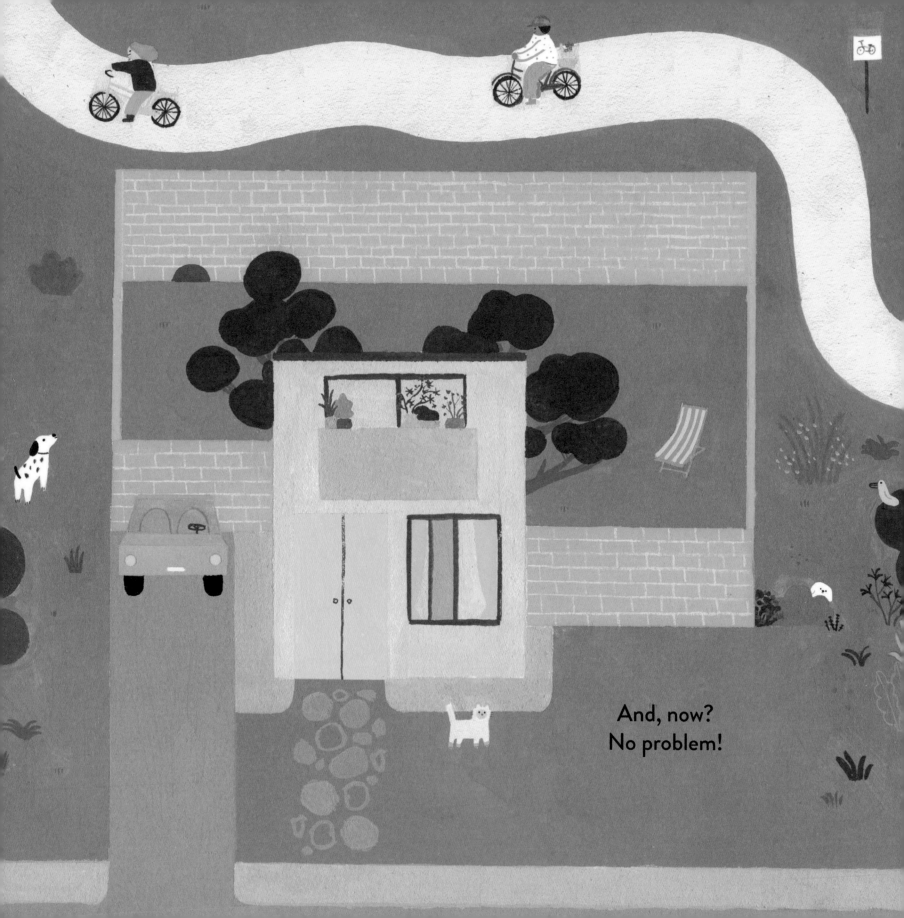

And, now?
No problem!

Olivia is an adventurer,

a tireless traveler,

an explorer without any—

Fear.

Well, maybe
just a little.

Not enough to stop her, though.

Or will it?

Sometimes, all you have to do is close your eyes . . .

and jump.

And if you do,
you can reach the
top of the world.

Who would've thought
she'd make it this far?!

The world outside isn't bad at all.

Aside from this.

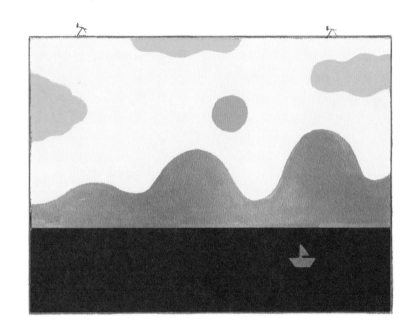